Mr. Nogginbody and the Childish Child

David Shannon

Norton Young Readers

An Imprint of W. W. Norton & Company
Independent Publishers Since 1923

For information about permission to reproduce selections from this book, write to Permissions, W. W. Norton & Company, Inc., 500 Fifth Avenue, New York, NY 10110

For information about special discounts for bulk purchases, please contact W. W. Norton Special Sales at specialsales@wwnorton.com or 800-233-4830

Library of Congress Cataloging-in-Publication Data

Names: Shannon, David, 1959– author, illustrator.

Title: Mr. Nogginbody and the childish child / David Shannon.

Description: First edition. | New York, NY : Norton Young Readers, an imprint of W. W. Norton & Company, [2020] | Audience: Ages 4–8. |

Summary: Mr. Nogginbody discovers that babysitting is much more difficult than he imagined, but also how much more fun it can be to act like a child than to be the grownup.

Identifiers: LCCN 2019052266 | ISBN 9781324004639 (hardcover) | ISBN 9781324004646 (epub)

Subjects: CYAC: Babysitters—Fiction. | Behavior—Fiction. | Humorous stories.

Classification: LCC PZ7.S52865 Mj 2020 | DDC [E]—dc23

LC record available at https://lccn.loc.gov/2019052266

W. W. Norton & Company, Inc., 500 Fifth Avenue, New York, N.Y. 10110

www.wwnorton.com

W. W. Norton & Company Ltd., 15 Carlisle Street, London W1D 3BS

1 2 3 4 5 6 7 8 9 0

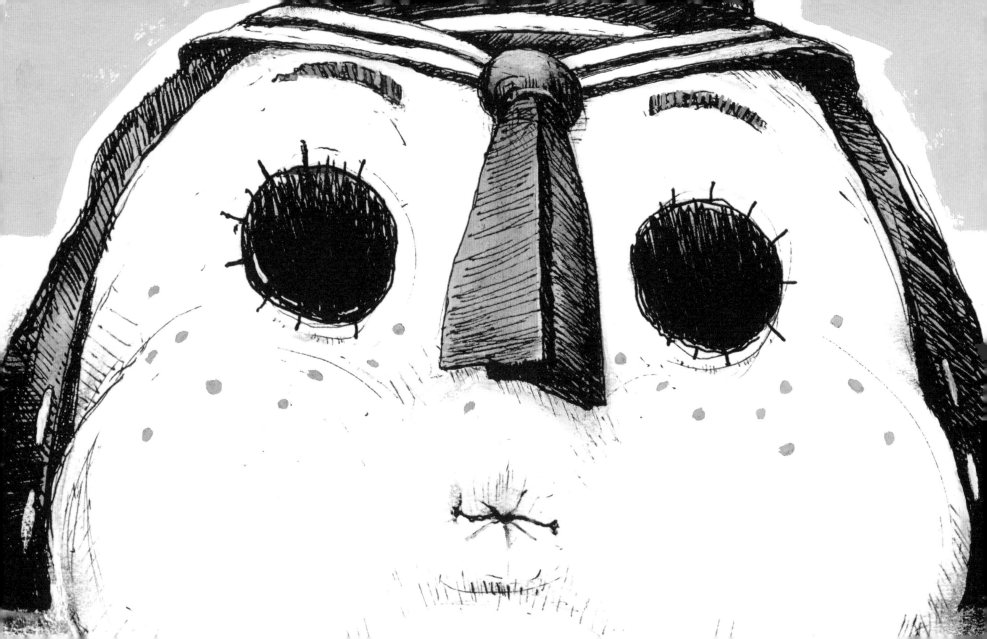

But, your mom said if I gave you a chocolate soda then you would do your homework.

Come on now,
turn off the TV.

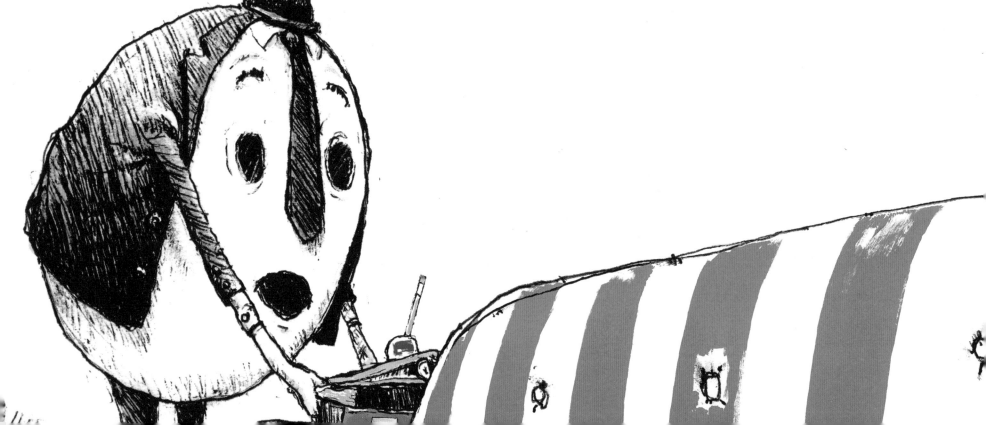

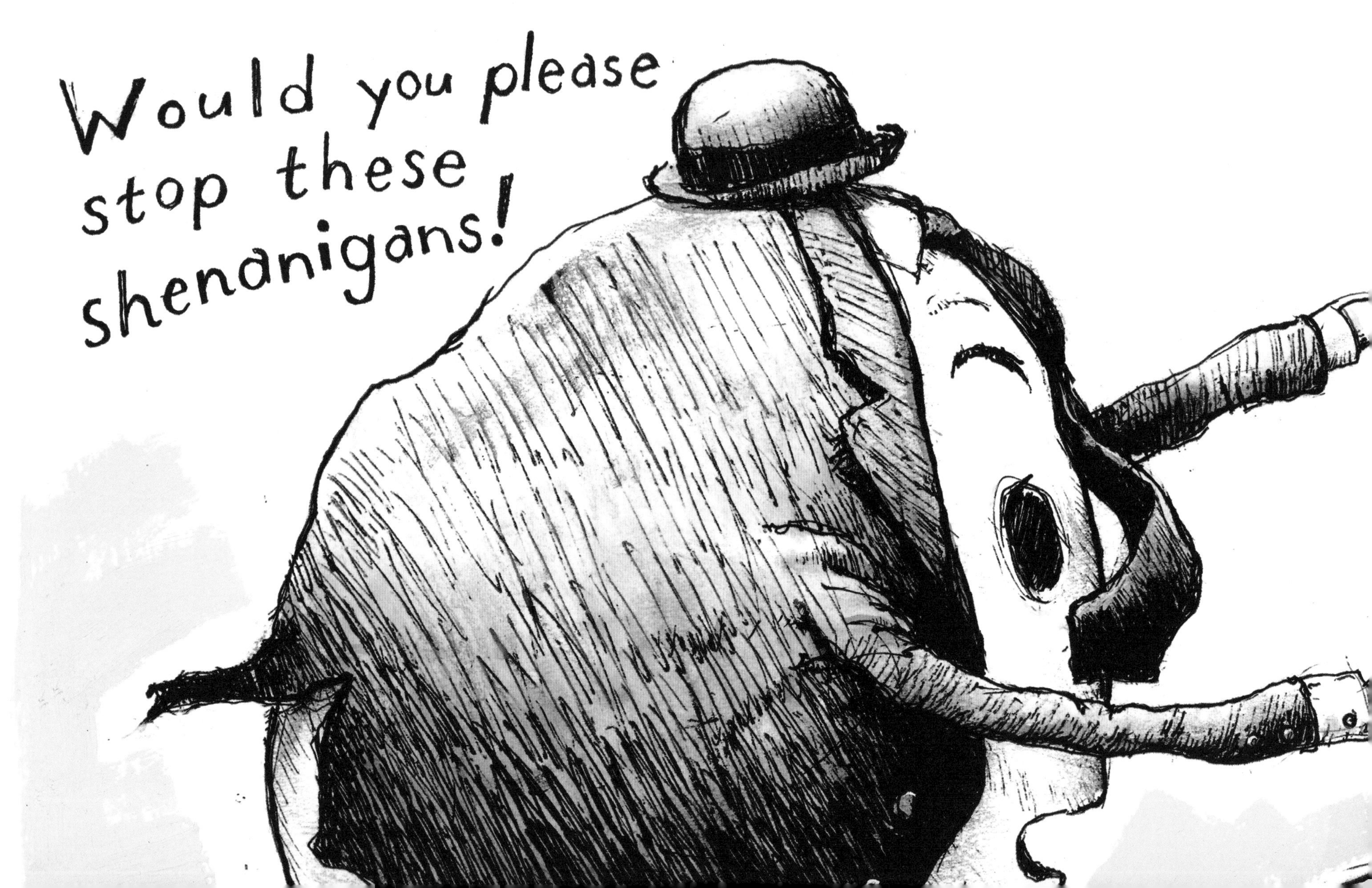
Would you please stop these shenanigans!

You broke your couch, too.

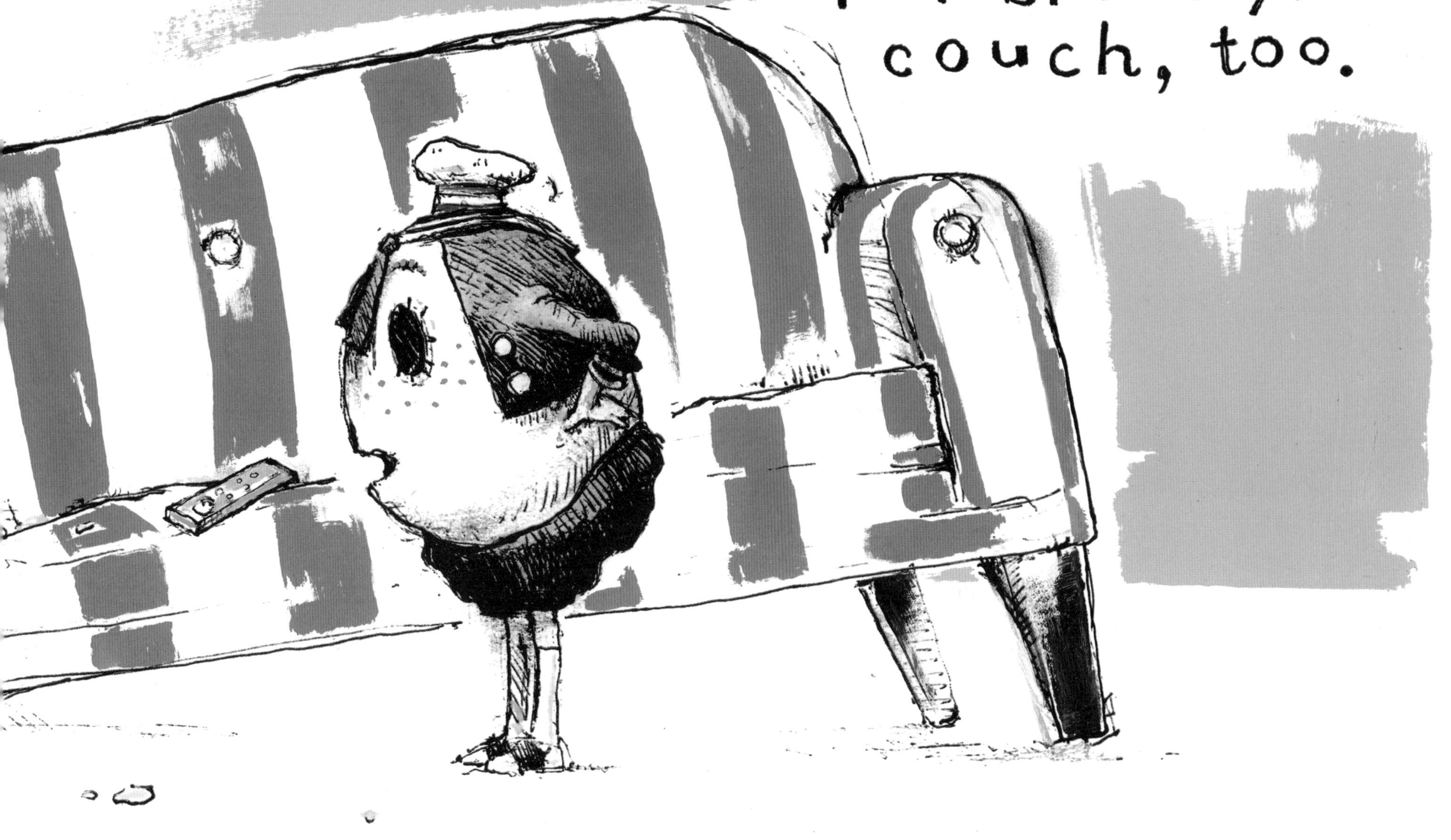

I'd be in deep doo-doo
if I did that.

Wait a minute—that would make me look rather childish.

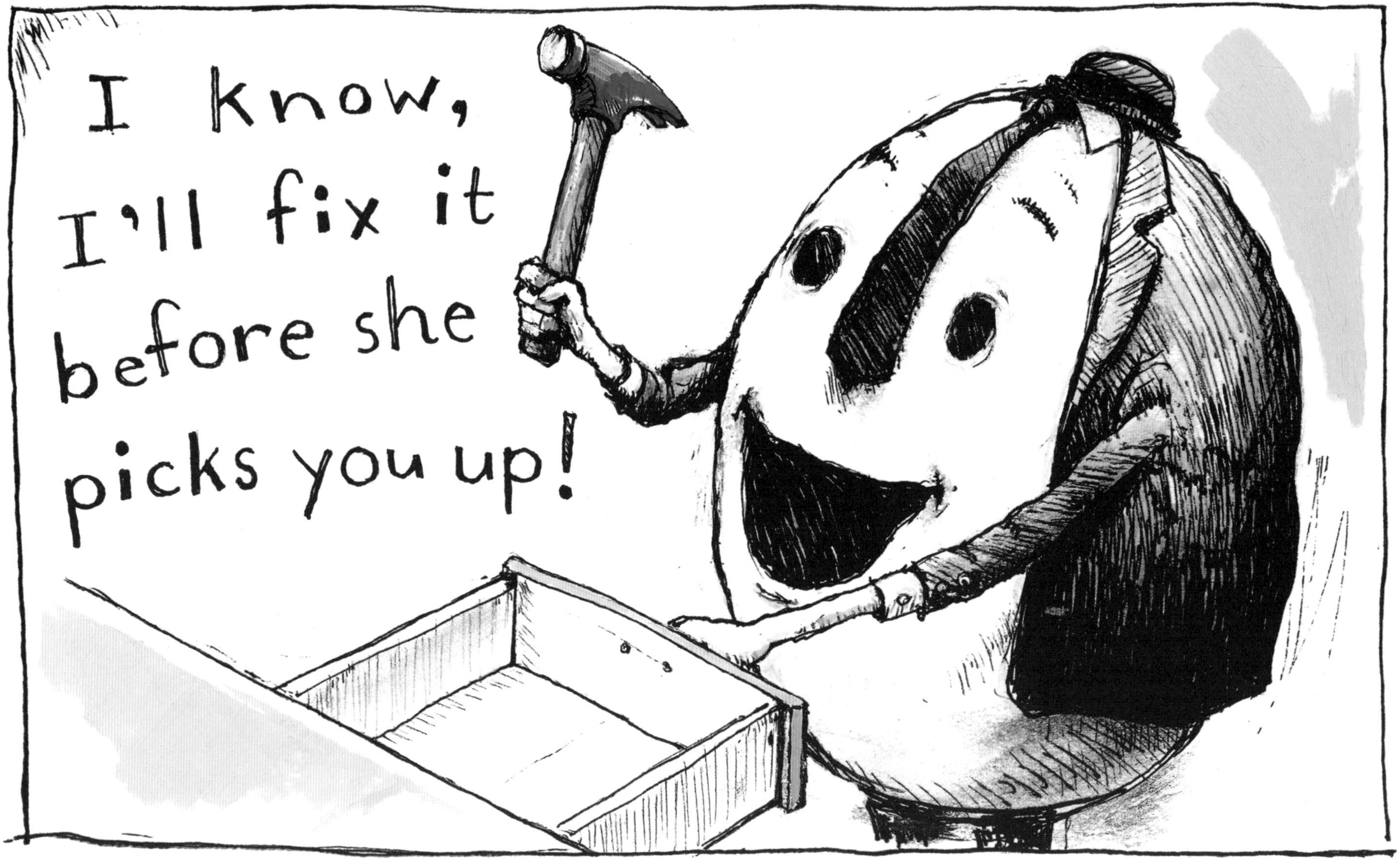
I know,
I'll fix it
before she
picks you up!